An I Can Read Book™

Minnie and Moo
The Night Before Christmas

Den s
Cazet

HarperCollins*Publishers*

For Alex and Jack—
Christmas and children
are one and the same.
Love,
Your aunties,
Minnie and Moo

HarperCollins®, 🏭®, and I Can Read Book® are
trademarks of HarperCollins Publishers Inc.

Minnie and Moo: The Night Before Christmas
Copyright © 2002 Denys Cazet
Printed in the U.S.A. All rights reserved.
www.harperchildrens.com

Library of Congress Cataloging-in-Publication Data is available.
ISBN 0-06-623752-1 — ISBN 0-06-623753-X (lib. bdg.)

1 2 3 4 5 6 7 8 9 10
❖
First Edition

'Twas the night before Christmas,

And all through the farm,

Not a creature was stirring,

Except in the barn.

Minnie and Moo sat at a small table.

Minnie poured hot cocoa.

Moo added some marshmallows.

5

"What's in that bag?" Minnie asked.

"Toys," Moo said. "Christmas toys
for the farmer's grandchildren."

"I saw the farmer hide them,"
said Minnie, cutting some fruitcake.

"But it's Christmas Eve," said Moo.

"Why didn't he come to get them?"

"That bag has been there for weeks,"

said Minnie. "Maybe he forgot again."

"He forgets every year," said Moo.

She put her cup down

and walked over to the window.

She looked at the rising moon.

It was bright on the white snow.

The farmhouse was dark.

"Those poor children," said Moo.

The farmer lay sleepless

With nary a wink:

*"Where **are** those presents?*

Under the sink?"

Moo pulled out a Santa Claus suit

and a big white beard

from an old trunk.

"Look at the picture in this book,"
said Moo. "See? These clothes
are the same ones Santa wears."
"Moo, have you been reading again?"
Minnie asked.
" '*Twas the Night Before Christmas*,"
Moo said. "By Clement Moose.
It's a how-to book
on delivering Christmas gifts."

Moo held up the book.

Minnie pointed at Moo.

"Moo . . . I know what you are doing.

You're thinking!

You're thinking of dressing up

as Santa and delivering those toys!"

"Not exactly," said Moo.

"This suit is too big for me.

I was thinking that you—"

"What! Me?"

"Minnie, we can't just drop the toys
on the front porch and run away."

"Why not?" asked Minnie.

"Because it's Christmas," said Moo.

Minnie sighed.

"Hand me the beard," she said.

When what to the world

Should suddenly appear,

But a wheel-less wheelbarrow,

And eight tiny reindeer?

Moo dragged an old wheelbarrow

across the barn floor.

"I can't find the wheel," said Moo.

Minnie looked at the wheelbarrow.

"Moo, are you sure—"

"Of course," said Moo.

She tied the wheelbarrow

to eight chickens standing in a row.

She tied plastic forks to their heads.

"See?" said Moo. "Now we have a sled

and eight tiny reindeer!"

Moo put on a big coat, boots, and a hat.

She put on a mustache.

"Moo," said Minnie, "*I'm* Santa Claus."

"I know," said Moo. "I'm Mrs. Claus."

"Hey, cows!" shouted the rooster.

"How come I didn't get any horns?

How come you only gave horns

to the chickens?

Am I the only one around here

who thinks about me all the time?"

Moo tied two plastic forks

to the rooster's head.

"That's better!" he grumbled.

The rooster strutted past the chickens.

"The boss always goes first," he said.

He tied himself to the front of the line.

Minnie stared at the rooster.

"Something's missing," she said.

The rooster looked around. "What?"

"I know," said Minnie.

She took out some lipstick

and painted the rooster's beak red.

"There," she said. "Now you're

Rudolph, the Red-Nosed Rooster."

"Ready!" said Moo.

"Open the barn doors!" Minnie yelled.

"Santa Claus is coming to town!"

To the top of the porch!

Look out for the wall!

Dash away, dash away,

Dash away all!

Moo pushed Minnie

to the edge of the hill.

"Go!" Minnie yelled.

Moo jumped into the wheelbarrow.

It sped downhill faster and faster.

"Make me proud, girls!"

shouted the rooster.

They hit a bump

and soared into the night.

"Flap, girls!" yelled the rooster.

"Flap! Flap! Flap!"

"Flap to the left!" Moo yelled.

"Look out for that tree!"

"Flap to the right!" Minnie shouted.

"Look out for the garage!"

"Make up your flappin' minds!"

the rooster yelled.

"Roof ahead!" Moo shouted.

"Coming down!" cried Minnie.

The wheelbarrow skipped

across the roof of the house.

Snow flew up into the air.

The wheelbarrow skidded

into the chimney and stopped.

The chickens lay in a pile.

The rooster dangled

over the edge of the roof.

Minnie didn't move.

Moo walked to the edge of the roof.

"See?" she said proudly.

"Just like in the book!"

The chimney's too small!

Should have checked it before,

No problem, don't worry,

They'll use the front door.

Moo looked down the chimney.

"The hole is too small," she said.

"We'll never get down there."

Moo turned around.

"Minnie? Where are you?"

"Down here," Minnie called softly.

"I fell off the roof!"

"Did you try the front door?"
Moo asked.

"It's locked," said Minnie.

"I have an idea," Moo said.

"Of course you do," Minnie muttered.

Moo pulled the rooster up.

"It's about time!" said the rooster.

"What were you waiting for—spring?"

"Sorry," said Moo.

"You should be," said the rooster.

"I'm so cold

I feel like a frozen rump roast."

Moo looked down the chimney.

"It's warmer down there," she said.

The rooster looked at Moo. "So?"

"So, why don't you go down
the chimney, get warm, and then
open the front door for Minnie?"

"What are you, crazy?" he asked.

"Please," Moo said. "The children—"

"The children?" said the rooster.

"Who cares about the children?
What about me? What about—"

Suddenly, the rooster slipped.

"Ack!" he cried, and disappeared.

Moo looked down the chimney.

"Thanks," she said.

Beneath the lights of the tree,

All the presents were spread,

While the little ones slept,

All nestled in bed.

Moo climbed down the ladder.

She dragged the bag of toys

to the front of the house.

The door creaked open.

Minnie gasped. "Who opened—"

"Shhh," said Moo. "It's the rooster."

"Ack," said the rooster.

"Moo, this is not the rooster.

The rooster is white.

The rooster has tail feathers.

Roosters don't ack.

That is a penguin," Minnie said.

"I *was* white," acked the rooster,

"before I got a free ride

down the chimney!"

The rooster waddled into the house.

"He even walks like a penguin,"

Minnie whispered.

"Minnie, please. Let's hurry!"

Minnie and Moo

put the presents under the tree.

They stopped.

"Listen," Moo whispered.

"Footsteps!"

The footsteps stopped.

The lights went on.

There stood Santa,

And the Mrs., too.

Do you think anyone knew

It was Minnie and Moo?

"It's Santa Claus!"

shouted the farmer's grandchildren.

They gave Minnie a big hug.

"And Mrs. Claus!" they yelled.

They hugged Moo.

The farmer's wife looked at the farmer.

"You sly old fox," she said.

"Pretending to forget

where you hid the children's gifts."

The farmer stared at Moo.

He stared at the mustache.

"Millie, how come

Mrs. Claus has a mustache?"

"You can't fool me," giggled Millie.

"I know who they really are!"

The farmer scratched his head.

"You do?" he asked.

"The Wilkersons," said Millie.

"I can tell by their noses!"

The grandchildren threw their arms

around the farmer.

"Oh, Grandpa," they said.

"This is the best Christmas ever!"

"Look!" shouted another.

"It's a penguin!"

"Oh, Grandpa." The children clapped.

"Our very own penguin!"

One of the children tied a ribbon

around the rooster's neck.

"Don't be shy," she said.

Minnie and Moo

slipped out the back door.

They made such a racket

And hullabaloo,

Jumped into the sleigh,

And away they all flew.

The children ran to the window.

"Look, Grandpa! Look, Grandma!"

they shouted. "There they go!"

More rapid than eagles,

They flew past the moon

While Santa played tuba,

And Mrs. Claus the bassoon.

"Hooray for Christmas!"

They were heard to proclaim,

"Children and Christmas

Are one and the same!"

Millie rested her hand
gently on the farmer's arm.
"John," she whispered.
"I don't think
that was the Wilkersons."